BREAK AND ENTER

LESLIE MCGILL

SADDLEBACK
EDUCATIONAL PUBLISHING

WH⚡TE L⚡GHTNING
BOOKS

BREAK AND ENTER

IGGY

ON THE RUN

QWIK CUTTER

REBEL

SCRATCH N' SNITCH

SADDLEBACK
EDUCATIONAL PUBLISHING
www.sdlback.com

Copyright © 2016 by Saddleback Educational Publishing
All rights reserved. No part of this book may be reproduced in any form or by any means, electronic or mechanical, including photocopying, recording, scanning, or by any information storage and retrieval system, without the written permission of the publisher. SADDLEBACK EDUCATIONAL PUBLISHING and any associated logos are trademarks and/or registered trademarks of Saddleback Educational Publishing.

ISBN-13: 978-1-68021-108-5
ISBN-10: 1-68021-108-0
eBook: 978-1-63078-425-6

Printed in Guangzhou, China
NOR/1015/CA21501554

20 19 18 17 16   1 2 3 4 5

STATS OF DWAYNE'S BREAK-INS

LIST OF WHAT DWAYNE EATS FROM STRANGERS' KITCHENS

- CHOCOLATE CHIP COOKIES
- PRETZELS
- LEFTOVER PIZZA
- CHERRY POPSICLES
- CHEEZ WHIZ ON CRACKERS
- FROZEN GRAPES

49% OF HOUSES IN THE NEIGHBORHOOD HAVE POOLS

51%

49%

MOST AFRAID OF MEETING WHEN BREAKING IN

AERIAL VIEW OF NEIGHBORHOOD

CHAPTER 1

MY FIRST BREAK-IN

Lots of people have weird hobbies. Like bug collecting. Mine? Breaking and entering.

I'm not bad. I don't break in to take stuff. That's what you're thinking, right?

It started when we moved here. Me and my mom. This city is full of apartments. What was inside each one? I wanted to find out.

Because my life sucks.

I wanted to borrow another life for a while.

Pretend I'm someone else. Trade my reality for make-believe.

Even if it was just for an afternoon.

"We'll get used to this," my mom said. "It'll take time."

"Yeah. Well, I want my old life back. I miss my friends. I miss the sun," I complained.

"This is for the best," she said.

End of story. I knew we couldn't go back. But, man, life was hard.

She knows moving here was tough on me. On both of us. We moved to get away from my father. He's not a nice guy.

To me, my mom, or anybody.

He's in prison right now. We wanted to start over. So we moved east.

It's been rough. My old life in California was all I knew. I'm trying to fit in here. But it's taking a while.

Other people's lives seem better than mine. I'm ready to trade.

I saw the open window walking to school. Anyone could have crawled through. Who leaves a first-floor window open? Especially in this part of town.

Crazy. They were lucky I was the one who discovered it. Instead of someone bad.

Three days in a row it was open. It was like an itch I couldn't scratch. Had to get inside. Couldn't let it go.

I needed a plan.

1. Go in the middle of the day
2. Ditch school right after lunch
3. Think of a lie to tell Mom in case school calls
4. Walk back to the apartment with the open window
5. Check around back for more open windows
6. If there isn't an open window, try to open one

7. But first make sure the coast is
   clear
8. Check for dogs

It was after lunch. Mom wouldn't find out I'd ditched school till later. Whatever. I'd make up something good. My mom is too trusting.

I walked to the apartment. Went around back. Didn't see any cars. But that doesn't mean anything. Most people take the bus to work.

The back gate squeaked. I freaked. Crouched down. Waited to see if anyone came out to investigate. After a minute I stood back up.

One window wouldn't move. Another had frosted glass. Hmm. The bathroom window? I pushed up against the frame. It moved up a couple inches.

"Here, boy! Come here, pup!" I called softly.

Lots of people here have dogs. No pit bull surprises, please. But no dog came.

No way could I pull myself up. It was too high.

There was a broken chair in the yard. I moved it under the window. It was the right height. I opened the window wider. Threw a leg over the windowsill. Shifted my weight. Pulled the other leg in. Dropped to the floor.

I was in.

CHAPTER 2

CRAZY HAPPY

It was a bathroom. Someone had showered recently. It smelled like soap. The towels were damp.

The apartment was quiet. Nobody home. A clock ticked somewhere. *Ticktock. Ticktock.*

I felt crazy happy. Better than that. I couldn't believe I'd done it.

I walked from room to room, touching things.

These people were normal. Not rich. But their lives seemed comfortable. The kids were messy, like me.

I knew I should probably hurry. But I wanted to look around first.

I went into the kitchen. Opened the refrigerator. There were leftovers inside. I took a whiff. Gross! Wasn't going to eat that!

What other food did these people have? I looked in a cupboard. Cookies! Score! I snagged five. Ate them as I walked into the living room.

There was a huge couch. It took up most of the room. It looked so inviting. I sat and kicked back, munching the cookies.

When would these people come home? It was getting late. I knew I should leave.

My stomach growled. Those cookies were calling my name. So I headed back to the kitchen. That's when I saw it. An old watch. Beat-up leather band. It was on the windowsill. Above the sink. It wasn't anything great. All scratched and dull.

No one would notice if it was gone. I stuck it in my pocket. A souvenir.

It was time to leave. *Ticktock. Ticktock.*

I walked back to the bathroom. Took a good look around. There were lots of bottles on the side of the sink. Perfumes. Lotions. I opened a couple. Smelled them. Put some lotion on my hands. Regretted it. It smelled girlie.

I climbed back out the window. Tried to pull it down after me. The lotion made my hands too slippery. I rubbed them on the front of my shirt.

I tried again. This time it came down.

I put the chair back where I'd found it and left through the gate.

My brain screamed *Run. Run, you fool.* But I knew that would attract attention. I walked home.

I unlocked the door to my apartment. Mom was in the kitchen. She came out, drying her hands on a towel.

"Dwayne Davis, it's about time you got home!" She put her hands on her hips. "Where have you been?"

Awesome. The school hadn't called. "At school," I lied. "Had to take care of something."

She sniffed. "What's that smell?" she asked. She came closer. She sniffed my shirt. She got a funny look on her face. Sort of a smile.

"What smell?"

"Smells like perfume," she said. "Is that what you had to take care of. She have a name?"

"Aw, Mom," I said, trying to sound embarrassed.

"That's okay," she said. "You can tell me about her when you're ready." She walked back into the kitchen. Then walked back out again. "Just her initials," she teased. "Just tell me that."

"B and E," I said. It was the first thing that came to mind. Hey, I wasn't lying. I'd spent the afternoon breaking and entering.

"Hmm," she said. "Brittany? Evans?"

"Mom!" I squirmed. Sometimes my mom is too much.

She laughed again and walked into the kitchen. I went into my room. Shut the door. Sat on my bed.

My poor clueless mother. She thought I had been hanging out with some girl. If she only knew the truth.

My bed was soft. My body felt tired. Like I had run a few miles. I must have been really tense.

The watch! I almost forgot. I pulled it from my pocket. Rubbed it a little. Then closed it in my palm. The metal felt warm.

I had to hide it. And I knew just the spot.

My treasure box was in my closet. Everything in there meant something to me.

Items in my treasure box.

1. My lucky penny from first grade, found

2. Bald eagle feather, found

3. Picture of my grandparents

4. Note from my favorite teacher

5. Letter from my mom, telling me Dad was out of our lives

6. Mini shampoo and lotion bottles
   from the only hotel I've ever
   stayed at

I opened the box. Looked at my treasures. Put the watch in carefully. I was glad I had taken it. It would always remind me of this day.

CHAPTER 3

BREAK-IN #2

I couldn't stop thinking about it. My visit. That's what I called it in my mind.

I knew it was illegal. But it felt so good. To be somebody else for a little while. And anyway, if I got caught? Community service all the way. I'm only fourteen.

I couldn't wait to do it again. Break and enter. It was never far from my mind.

About two weeks later, I get my chance. On my way to school, I pass this apartment. Never seen anyone. But on this day the building door opens. A man and a woman walk out. A window on the first floor is open.

Wide open.

I had to go in. That meant ditching school. I'd have some fast talking to do.

I walked to the end of the block. Turned right. Then turned around to watch. Nobody noticed me.

There was an alley behind the building. I walked down it. Opened the back gate. Ha! Just as I thought. One of the back windows was open too. Just like in front.

So careless. People like this deserve to be robbed. It was practically an invitation.

I looked around for something to climb on. There was a blue recycling crate. It was filled with empty cans. I dumped them out. They made a terrible noise. I froze. Waited a while. Nothing. All clear.

I stood on the crate. Stuck my head through the window.

"Here, pup!" I called. "Come here, boy!" You can never be too careful about mean dogs.

There was no response. I climbed over the windowsill.

This was a bedroom. I dropped to the floor. Looked around. The bed was made. There was a shirt on a chair. Otherwise, the room was very tidy.

I liked these people. Careless about their window. But neat.

I had picked a good place for my visit. I felt happy. Decided to spend the whole day here.

I snooped. Noticed how clean everything was. Walked into the kitchen. It smelled like toast. The toaster was warm.

There was a full cup of tea on the counter. It was warm too.

Odd.

I walked into another bedroom. This one was messier. The bed was unmade. There were lots of photographs on the walls. Old-fashioned pictures. Like from another time, or maybe another country.

There was a metal walker by the bed. I wonder who used it. The people seemed to be walking fine when they left.

I moved over to the dresser. Opened the top drawer. Girlie underwear. Yuck. The next drawer had sweaters. I pulled out the bottom drawer. It was filled with junk. Necklaces that looked like a kid had made them. Notes addressed to Grandma.

I reached into the farthest corner. There was a dark wooden box. I pulled it out.

Inside was an old-fashioned pocket watch. I took it out. "Hello," I said. People should find safer places to hide their stuff.

I put it in my pocket.

Under the watch were some large silver coins. I looked at them closely. Silver dollars. Never seen any of those before. I put them in my pocket too.

There was also a gold ring. It barely fit my pinky. I would keep it. Serves them right for leaving valuables in the house, I thought.

I closed the box. Put it back in the drawer. I

tried to close the drawer. But it stuck. I had to jam it hard with both hands. Finally, it slid back into place.

I started to leave the bedroom. That's when I saw the closet door. I turned the handle. It wouldn't budge.

That was strange. Closet doors aren't usually locked. I bent down to get a closer look. I couldn't see a keyhole. It had to be stuck.

I turned it harder. It moved a little.

All of a sudden, the door flew open. It knocked me back.

An old woman fell out. Screaming.

CHAPTER 4

A DANGEROUS GAME

Help! Somebody help me!"

I was too shocked to say anything.

The woman was hysterical. She screamed again and again.

Stop, lady. Stop, I thought. I put my hand over her mouth. She tried to bite me.

"I'm not going to hurt you, lady," I said. "Just stop screaming."

She quit screaming. She stood still. Her eyes looked terrified.

"I'm not a bad guy," I said. "I just wanted to look around." I loosened my hand a little. "I want to let you go. Will you promise not to scream anymore?"

She nodded.

I took my hand away slowly. "Okay, that's better," I said. "Are you okay? Did I hurt you?"

She shook her head.

"Do you want your cup of tea?"

She looked at me like I was wack. She shook her head again. I didn't blame her.

"May I have my walker?" she asked.

"Of course," I said. I handed it to her.

She grabbed it with both hands.

I stepped aside.

The walker was between us. She just looked at me. She still looked frightened. And maybe a little mad.

"Would you be more comfortable in the living room?" I asked.

She nodded.

I gestured for her to go first. She walked down the hall. I followed her. When we got to the living room, I stopped.

"I'm not going to stay," I said. "I just wanted to see inside. If you're okay, I think I'll go."

She didn't move. I figured it would be a while before she calmed down.

"I guess I'll just leave by the front door," I said. I walked in that direction.

"Young man," she snapped.

I turned.

"I want you to give me what you took from my drawer."

"I didn't take anything."

"Yes, you did. And I want them back. Those things belonged to my parents. They mean a great deal to me. More than they will ever mean to you. And I want them back."

I hesitated. Then pulled out the watch. Put it on the coffee table. Put the ring on top of it.

"Okay, that's it. I'm leaving," I said, turning for the door.

"All of it!" she said. Her voice was hard. This was not an old lady to mess with.

I reached into my pocket. I pulled out the silver coins. I put them on the table with the other things.

"Is that it?" she asked.

I showed her my empty pockets. "Empty," I said. I started for the door. "Don't call the cops," I said. "I didn't take anything. I wasn't going to hurt you. I didn't know anyone was home. I just like visiting."

"Young man," she said sternly.

I waited.

"I could have been standing there with a shot-gun," she said. "I could have blown your head off. No one would have blamed me. You're playing a dangerous game. You need to stop."

I nodded. "Yeah, I know," I said. "Have a good day, okay?"

I opened the door. Walked out. And heard it close quietly behind me. Then I left the building.

I was careful walking home. Figured she was going to call the cops. I ducked through backyards and alleys.

I got to the corner of my street. Looked down the block. No sign of anything wrong. I listened for a moment. A bus passed by. I could hear a car radio.

I got to my house. Went inside. Walked straight to my room. I put my hand in my pocket. And pulled out a silver dollar.

Yeah, I lied to the old lady. Kept one of her coins. I needed my souvenir.

She had a lot of them. She wouldn't miss one.

What the old lady had said was true. I was playing a dangerous game. Would she call the cops? ID me?

This visit went badly. It could have gone even worse. I could be dead. I knew I should stop.

The problem was, I liked it. Stepping over a

windowsill into someone else's life? Awesome. Getting caught by the old lady? Meh, didn't bother me.

I couldn't wait to do it again.

CHAPTER 5

REALITY SUCKS

At dinner my mom chatted about friends she's made at work. Bernice and Tara. She wants to have them over for dinner.

She wants me to make some friends too. She made me join the basketball club at school. It's okay. I don't hate it.

Basketball just doesn't compare to my new hobby.

Breaking and entering.

Leaving my real life behind. Being in some-one else's life for a while.

I wanted to do it again. For a couple of weeks, I watched for another chance. I didn't see any other places that looked promising.

And then I got busy with school. The eighth grade teachers assigned some long-term projects. I had lots of homework.

Typical homework list.

1. Algebra, 2 worksheets
2. U.S. history, textbook reading
   plus primary source material
   (Freedom Riders, man, those
   dudes were the bomb)
3. Science, lab reports
4. English, expository writing assignment
   (dont fear the essay, people)
5. English, reading assignment (right
   now it's Shakespeare)

But I never forgot how it felt to be inside someone else's life.

One afternoon, everything changed. I took a different path home.

On my way I saw an alley. I could see the backs of apartments. Did a double take. Couldn't believe what I saw. Someone had left a ladder up. It rested against the back of one of the buildings.

I crossed over to the alley and looked up. A window was open on the second floor. It was near where the ladder was propped.

Hadn't planned to make a visit today. But this was too hard to resist.

I put my backpack on the ground. Looked around. I couldn't see anyone.

You can never be too careful. Someone could be watching from another apartment.

I climbed up quickly. Shoved up the screen. Pushed the window up farther. I started to climb over the sill.

Then I remembered my rule about dogs. "Here, boy," I called. "Come on, pup!"

I waited a minute. No response. I pushed up a window shade. Slipped under it.

I was in! It was a bedroom. The bed wasn't made. Clothes were all over the bed and the floor. Slobs lived here for sure.

I pulled the shade back down to hide the window. Listened for a minute. Couldn't hear anything.

"Hello?" I called out. I didn't want to be surprised by another old lady in a closet.

The apartment was completely quiet. No one was home.

I walked into the bathroom. The top was off the toothpaste tube. Damp towels were on the floor. I hung up the towels. Put the top on the toothpaste.

Next was the living room. Game controllers were on the floor. There were five empty glasses on the coffee table. Several empty bags of potato chips. Candy wrappers.

Unbelievable.

This was disgusting. I'm no clean freak. But who could enjoy visiting a pigsty?

I put the controllers on the shelf by the game consoles. I took the glasses into the kitchen. Washed them. Cleaned up some dirty pans on the stovetop.

I went back into the bedroom. Some of the dresser drawers were open. I closed them all, but one was stuck. It was filled with big clunky necklaces. Ugly. But someone obviously liked them. A lot.

I bent down to see what was keeping the drawer from closing. A small red box was sticking up in the back.

I pulled it out. Inside was a ring with a blue stone. It looked expensive.

For a moment I hesitated. If it was expensive, the owner might call the police.

But they might just think they lost it in this clutter. I put it in my pocket. Shut the drawer.

I looked around. Clothes were everywhere. Time to straighten up.

Something on the floor caught my eye. I pushed some clothes aside to see. There were boxes on the floor. One was filled with cell phones. Another was filled with tablets and laptops.

I pulled out an iPhone. It was a newer model. I turned it on. Couldn't get a signal. I pulled out another phone. It didn't work either.

Maybe whoever lived there just had bad luck with phones. Then I realized what was going on. No one had that many broken phones. These had been disabled. Their owners had made sure nobody could use them. Probably right after this guy stole them.

I knew I had to get out. Whoever lived here was a thief. Last thing I wanted was to get caught with all this stolen stuff.

I headed for the door of the apartment. I reached for the doorknob.

Right then the door opened. It nearly hit me in the forehead.

I don't know who was more surprised. Me. Or the guy holding the door.

He stood in the doorway. His body blocked my escape. He put his hand into the waistband of his pants. Pulled out a gun.

He pointed it at me.

"Son, you have about five seconds to explain what you're doing in my apartment," he said. "Starting now."

CHAPTER 6

GET OUT!

I was beyond scared. Couldn't speak. Started a few times, but nothing came out.

"I ... I ... I ... don't shoot!" I said.

"I'm waiting," he answered. "Talk."

"My aunt told me to meet her here. She had a cleaning job. She asked me to help her."

Lame. But it was the first thing that came to mind.

"What's her name?" the man asked.

I drew a blank. "Nala," I blurted out.

The guy looked skeptical. "Nala?" he said.

"Yeah," I said.

"How'd you get in?" the man asked.

"The door was open," I lied. "I figured she had to step out for a minute. So I started cleaning. She hasn't come back yet. I'm getting worried. I've been here a long time."

"She's not here because you've got the wrong apartment," the man snapped. He looked around quickly. "You cleaned this place up?" he asked.

I nodded.

"How long have you been here?" he asked.

"A while," I said. "I kept thinking she was coming. I heard you at the door. I thought it was her."

"Show me what you did," he said. He motioned with the gun.

I walked toward the kitchen. He looked at the dishes in the dish rack. He touched one. He rubbed his fingers on his pants to dry them off.

He motioned with the gun again. We walked

down the hall. He looked into the bathroom. He stepped into the bedroom. "You go into that closet?" he asked.

I shook my head. "I put all the clothes over there," I said, pointing toward the basket.

He looked at the basket. Then he looked back at the closet.

"You sure you didn't open that closet door?" he asked.

"I'm sure."

Right then, a breeze moved the window shade slightly. The window was still wide open. I hadn't shut it when I climbed in.

He was looking at the closet door. He didn't notice.

"Son, I don't know what your game is," he said, turning around. "I don't believe for a minute that you have an aunt Nala. But someone cleaned this place up. It wasn't me or my girlfriend. So I'm gonna let you go."

I let my breath out.

"Anything you saw here? You better keep it to yourself," he continued. "You understand?"

I nodded.

"Get out of here," he said. "I'd better not ever see or hear from you again. Understand?"

I nodded and practically ran. Okay, I did run. All the way home.

Along the way, I passed a woman. She was wearing a huge clunky necklace. For sure she was the woman from the apartment.

I got inside my place. My mother had just gotten home. She had been out with her friends from work. She was full of gossip. She talked on and on.

When she took a breath, I told her I had homework. I went into my room. Pushed the shirts in my closet to the side. Grabbed the metal box. Put the ring in.

I lay on my bed and thought about my day.

It had been a really, really close call. That was one bad guy.

He ran a risk letting me go. All I would have to do was call the cops. Tell them just where the stolen stuff was located. Thank goodness he let me go.

I'd been lucky. Lucky twice, actually. Once with the old lady. And again today. I knew I should stop. Odds were, I was going to get caught.

But the danger was adding to the fun. I had started these visits just to see other people's lives. Escape from my own. Breaking in was exciting enough. But getting away from the old lady and the crook? Talking my way out of danger made this even better.

My new skill set:

1. Thinking fast under pressure
2. Talking my way out of danger
3. Finding another way out when faced with an obstacle
4. Fixing my mistakes

I stood up to start my homework.

Oh. No. I. Didn't. My heart was pounding.

I'd made the biggest mistake of all. One that couldn't be fixed.

I'd left my backpack in the backyard of the building.

It was filled with papers from school. My name and address were on some of them.

If he found my backpack, he would know who I am.

And where to find me.

CHAPTER 7

I KNOW WHO YOU ARE

That night I didn't sleep. Kept thinking about my backpack. Thinking about the papers inside. Papers I never got signed.

Papers that included my name and address.

My textbooks were in there. Along with the English journal I'd been keeping. I had to get those back.

I could just picture what happened. The window shade moves in and out with the breeze.

The guy goes to close the window. Discovers the open screen.

Looks out and sees the ladder.

Looks down and sees the backpack.

Realizes how I got into the apartment. And knows I was lying.

And then he …

Does what exactly? Imagining his next step kept me awake. He'd pointed a gun at me once. Seemed willing to use it. He was probably planning my murder right now.

But maybe he didn't notice the backpack. Maybe he just shut the window. Didn't look down. Maybe it was still there.

I had to get it back.

The next morning I got up before my alarm. I got dressed and walked into the kitchen. "I have some stuff to do at school this morning. So I'm going to head out early," I said.

"Okay," my mom said, sipping her coffee. "See you tonight."

I headed for the door.

"Wait!" she called out. "Isn't there something you forgot?"

I walked back to the kitchen. I gave her a hug. "Bye," I said.

"Not that. But I'll take it," she said. "Didn't you forget to make your lunch?"

Busted.

I'd hoped she wouldn't notice. I make my lunch every day. Unfortunately, my lunch bag was in the backpack.

"Must be losing my mind," I said, shaking my head. "Still got that salami?"

"Got some the other day," my mother said.

I opened the refrigerator. I took out salami, cheese, and mustard.

"I need a bag," I said.

"A bag?" she asked.

"I left my backpack at school," I said. "My lunch bag is in it." I braced myself for her reaction.

"You what?" she asked incredulously. "What about your homework?"

Only one excuse would calm her down. "Yeah, forgot to tell you," I said, trying to look embarrassed. "I played a little basketball with some guys yesterday. After school. I must have left it on the court."

It worked. She was thrilled that I might have made some friends. "You did?" my mother said excitedly. "Who are these boys? Do you like them? Do they live nearby? See? I told you the basketball club was a good thing."

She handed me a bag as she fired off her questions.

"They were just some guys. They were okay," I said. That's usually enough to satisfy her. "Now, I'm out."

"Be good!" she called after me.

"Always am," I lied.

Lying to my mom sucks. She's so desperate for me to be happy here. But lying about having friends isn't terrible. And it's kinder than telling her the truth.

I walked toward the apartment. I could see the rear of the building. Amazingly, the ladder was still there. I looked up at the window I had crawled through. It was shut.

I walked into the backyard. No way. My backpack was right where I'd left it. On the ground at the base of the ladder.

Nobody was around. I looked up at the window. I half-expected to see the man. The window was empty.

I grabbed my backpack. Raced out of there. Didn't care who saw me. I was just a kid running to school.

When I was about a block away, I unzipped it. Looked inside. My textbooks were there. My English journal too.

I shoved my lunch bag inside. And hurried on to school. It felt like everything was there. Maybe the guy hadn't found the backpack after all.

I took my seat just as the late bell rang. I slowly started to relax. I quietly opened my backpack. Took out my textbooks, journal, and lunch. At the bottom were all the old papers.

But something else was there. A new sheet of paper. It was folded into a tight square. My name and address were written on the outside.

It hadn't been there yesterday.

I pulled it out. Opened it. Straightened out all the folds.

The message was short.

I KNOW WHO YOU ARE.
I KNOW WHERE YOU LIVE.

There was no signature. None was needed. The picture of the smoking gun was enough.

I knew it was from the guy in the apartment.

CHAPTER 8

GAME OVER

I was done. No more breaking and entering. I got the message. Loud and clear.

Talk about being tense. I could hardly leave the house. I felt safer in school. It helped that I had gotten to know some kids.

My mom's plan had worked after all. Some of the basketball guys were in my U.S. history class. I had started sitting with them at lunch. They were okay.

My mom hadn't noticed the changes in me.

She was all caught up in gossip from work. Usually I just tuned her out.

"Bernice told me the most amazing story today," my mother said at dinner. "You're going to love this. She didn't mean it to be funny. But it was hard not to laugh."

I poured myself some milk. Sighed inside. Sometimes my mom's stories went on for a while.

"So what happened?" I asked.

"Well, she's sure her boyfriend is cheating on her. He sounds like a loser. She deserves better. His name is Michael. Michael Stevens. She caught him in the most amazing lie."

Boring. Who cares about these people? "What'd he say?" I asked.

"Well, apparently, Michael had some woman at their place," she continued. "While Bernice was at work. The woman must have been some sort of clean freak. Bernice came home. Found the apartment completely clean. The woman had cleaned it top to bottom."

This was interesting. "He hadn't done it?" I asked.

"No. He said he came home. Found it clean. Can you believe it? As if Bernice would fall for that story! It had to be some woman. No one breaks in and cleans."

I do! Or at least I did. I broke into an apartment and cleaned it. Strange that someone else did the same thing.

I wasn't laughing. Mom didn't notice.

"He claimed to have caught the guy," she continued. "Said it was some kid. Some story about being in the wrong apartment. Bernice doesn't believe it for a minute."

At this point I was barely breathing.

"And whoever was really in the apartment stole some jewelry. A ring that had belonged to Bernice's mother. She is furious," Mom said, shaking her head. "Bad enough that he brought a woman to their place. But to have that woman steal Bernice's ring? The ring is probably long gone by now. She kicked Michael out that very night."

This was awful. Michael was telling the truth. There was no other woman.

It was me. I had broken into my mother's friend's apartment. What a terrible coincidence.

I needed some time to process this. I stood up. Picked up the dishes. And took them into the kitchen.

"So we should be careful to always lock up," my mother called out. "Although"—she gave a little laugh—"I don't know. I wish someone would break in here and clean."

I forced myself to laugh. I put the dishes in the dishwasher. And headed for my room. I needed to think.

"Oh, Dwayne?" my mother called.

"What?" I answered.

"Just wanted to let you know. I invited Bernice and Tara over for dinner Friday night. I can't wait for you to meet them."

I groaned. I couldn't believe this.

"Great!" I lied. Just great.

I reviewed all the ways I messed up.

1. I break into old lady's apartment
2. Get caught by old lady
3. I break into Bernice's apartment (one of two friends Mom has made since we moved here)
4. Steal Bernice's mom's ring
5. Michael catches me (he has a gun! he is a thief!)
6. Bernice thinks Michael's a cheater
7. Michael gets dumped
8. Michael has to move out
9. And I lie to my mom—a lot

Michael has lost his girlfriend. And his apartment. He knows I stole the ring.

He knows who I am.

He knows where I live.

He has a gun.

I am so dead.

CHAPTER 9

MAKE IT RIGHT

How to make things right? Give the ring back. I didn't want it. It was a souvenir. I was never going to wear it. Or give it to anyone. Or sell it.

Give it all back. Bernice's ring. The watch. The silver dollar. I was disgusted with myself for stealing. That's not who I am.

The watch and the coin could wait. I had to give Bernice back her ring.

I wished she hadn't kicked Michael out of their apartment. I could have gone over there.

Given him the ring. Could have stopped by when she was at work. It would have been awkward. But it would have made things right.

Where was he now? It was my fault.

I thought about giving the ring back to Bernice. She would be at my house Friday night.

"Hey, Bernice. Nice to meet you. I broke into your apartment. Weird, huh? I took your ring. And cleaned the place up."

Nah. Couldn't do it. Not to my mom's friends. They would hate her. And my mom would kill me. Bernice would probably call the cops.

I had to find another way.

"My mother told me you lost this. I found it on the sidewalk."

"I saw a guy selling this. I bought it for you."

Totally lame. I needed another idea.

What about dropping the ring into her purse? The risk was too high. If I got caught, it would just make things worse.

What about slipping the ring into her pocket? She'd find it later. Maybe think she had left it there herself.

Not a good plan. Too many ways I could fail. Bernice might not have pockets. She might catch me putting the ring inside. Or Tara or my mother would see me do it.

It was also really cowardly. But I didn't have another idea.

By the time Friday came, I was a wreck. My mom didn't notice. She had too much nervous energy. She hurried around cooking dinner for her friends. I offered to set the table.

"Three places or four?" I asked.

"Four," she answered. "I hope you'll eat with us."

"Sure," I said, trying to sound enthusiastic. "I can't wait to meet your friends."

She put some rolls on the table. Kissed me on the forehead. "You are so sweet," she said. "I'm glad you want to meet them. They want to meet you too."

I felt guilty. Didn't really care about meeting her friends. Just wanted to get rid of the evidence. I already had the ring in my pocket. I kept touching it.

At six thirty the buzzer rang. And there they were. Bernice and Tara. Both women were wearing jackets. I was excited. My plan might work.

I offered to hang up their jackets. My mother said to just throw them on her bed.

I carried the jackets down the hall. I threw Tara's on the bed. I looked at the front of Bernice's jacket. And you know what? No pockets. I looked at the inside. No pockets.

Who wears a jacket without pockets? Who makes a jacket without pockets? I shook my head in disgust.

My mother called me for dinner. I followed the two women to the table. They were gabbing and laughing away.

I felt more desperate. Picked at my food. When we were done, I cleared the table. My chances of making things right were slipping away.

As I left I heard Tara say, "So, give us the latest. Have you seen Michael? Do you know where he's living now?"

I stopped in the hallway. I strained to hear Bernice's answer.

"I saw him all right," she said grimly. "He moved back into his old place. It's such a dump! I followed him a couple of times. I want to catch him with his new girlfriend."

Poor Michael. Doubt he actually has another girlfriend.

"Where is his place?" my mom asked.

"Over on Vine Street," Bernice said. "Where it dead ends."

I know Vine Street. It's near the rec center. I've walked by there a few times.

Just like that another plan formed. I could try

to find Michael's apartment on Vine. Then I could give him the ring.

The conversation moved on to work gossip.

This new plan might work.

CHAPTER 10

AN OPEN WINDOW

Mom had to work on Saturday. Some special project. Said she would be home after lunch. She was long gone when I got up.

I poured myself some cereal. Then put on some clothes and left the apartment. I walked toward Vine Street. Vine Street was mostly old houses. Most were run-down. Some of the homes were boarded up.

I walked down the street. Looked carefully at

each house. I had no way of knowing which one was Michael's. No one was outside.

Toward the end, the row of houses stopped. There was an alley that led through to the next street. On the other side of the alley was a duplex. Two houses that shared an inside wall. The house nearest the alley was boarded up.

The other house looked like it should be boarded up. The paint on the front door had peeled. The bare wood had warped so the door hung crooked. The concrete steps were crumbling.

I don't know what made me walk down the alley. But I did. I walked about twenty yards. Turned. Looked at the back of the duplex.

The back was a mess. Garbage spilled out of trash cans. The garbage looked like it had been there for a while. Animals had ripped open some of the bags.

I hoped I didn't see a rat. I hate rats.

Does anyone even live here?

And then I saw it.

An open window.

One of the windows on the first floor was open wide. The frame was crooked. It looked like the window had gotten stuck.

Not again. I wanted to go in.

What was wrong with me? My previous visits hadn't gone well. Clearly, I was not good at this. The last one nearly got me killed. It got a guy busted. Made him lose his girlfriend. His apartment too.

But a wide-open window? That would be hard for anyone to resist. Anyone like me. Lonely. Sad. Missing my old life just a little.

I gave myself a shake. I was done with breaking and entering. It had gotten me in too much trouble already.

Where was Michael? I was there because of him. To give the ring back. To try to make things right.

So far my walk had been unsuccessful. I still

didn't know which house he lived in. And I sure wasn't going to start knocking on doors.

I started to head for home. But then I took one last look around. Checked the nearby houses. Tried to determine if anyone could see the open window.

But of course, it wouldn't matter even if they could. After all, I wasn't going to break in. I was done with that. Done.

At the end of the alley was a path. It led to some fields. I walked down the path. I was on the playing fields behind the rec center. Some little kids played soccer. I passed a basketball court. Some guys were playing a game. I recognized them from school.

"Hey, Dwayne!" one of them called out. "How you doing?"

It was Q. One of the guys in my U.S. history class. He's in the ball club at school too. Don't know his real name. He's okay. We're sort of friends.

"You want to play? We need someone," he

said. He tossed me the ball. "You're on my team with Alex and Jordan."

The guys nodded at me. I like basketball. Pretty good at it too. Even scored a couple points. Mostly I tried to pass the ball. We played for about an hour. Then some other guys wanted the court. We finished our game.

Jordan headed up the path. I wanted to walk that way too. Wanted to check out that house again. But I didn't want to walk with anyone. I needed to check it out alone.

I walked with Q and Alex in the opposite direction. When we got to the corner, they both turned right. I said goodbye and turned left. I headed back toward the alley.

The house looked just the same. The window was still open. Anyone who saw it could break in.

Anyone but me, of course. I was done with breaking and entering. Done.

CHAPTER 11

BIG MISTAKE

Just keep walking, Dwayne, I told myself. Before I knew it, I passed the first place I'd visited. The place where I ate the cookies. Stole the watch.

The front window of the apartment was closed. Bet you a million dollars the back window was closed too. They'll probably never leave a window open again. Ever.

I walked past a light pole in front of their building. Stopped. Turned back. Someone had put a sign on the pole.

LOST OR STOLEN MAN'S WATCH
SENTIMENTAL VALUE!
PLEASE RETURN
NO QUESTIONS ASKED
REWARD!!!

Underneath was an address and phone number.

I *knew* that watch. It was in a metal box in my closet.

I wished I hadn't taken it. It meant nothing to me. But it meant something to someone.

I put the number on the sign into my phone.

First Bernice's ring. Now the watch. That just left the silver dollar.

Breaking in was one thing. Taking stuff had put me in another league. I needed to return the items I stole. Then my conscience would be clear.

By the time I got home, my mother was there too.

"Where you been? You're all sweaty," she said.

"I met up with a few guys from school. We shot some hoops at the rec center," I said.

She clapped her hands in delight. "Oh, baby, that's so great!" she said. "I wanted this move to work out. I've got some friends. Now you do too. Life is good, isn't it?"

No, I thought. Life won't be good until I find Michael. A guy who carries a gun in his waistband. I need to return the ring I stole from his girlfriend. One of your new friends.

"It is good," I agreed. "By the way, how's Bernice doing?" I wanted to change the subject.

"I'm beginning to think Bernice is a little crazy," she said. Mom shook her head. "She's started following her ex-boyfriend. She's sure he has a new girlfriend."

"She's stalking him?" I asked with a laugh.

"I know, right?" my mom said. "I almost feel sorry for him."

Poor Michael. He's done a lot of bad things. Stole cell phones and laptops. Stuck a gun in my face. But he didn't do what Bernice is accusing him of.

"What's Michael's job anyway?" I asked. I wondered if my mother knew he was a thief.

"He fixes cell phones and laptops," she answered. "Apparently, he's really good at it."

No way. Michael's stash of electronics was legit. So why the gun?

"Guess he's been robbed before," my mother said. "He even has a permit to carry a gun. Scares Bernice half to death."

It was like she read my mind.

Then she looked thoughtful. "I don't believe a stranger cleaned his apartment. It doesn't make sense. But he swears there's no new girlfriend. Who knows what the truth is?"

I had to find Michael. I knew the truth. Maybe I couldn't make things right with him and Bernice. But I could at least give back the ring.

I had a new to-do list in my mind.

1. Find Michael

2. Give back Bernice's ring

3. Call the number from the light
   pole

4. Give back the watch

5. Go back to the old lady

6. Give back the silver dollar

7. Go back to the run-down house

8. Break and enter

Old habits die hard. I was going in. Just thinking about it gave me a thrill.

Monday morning, I slipped the ring into my pocket. Brought along the watch and the silver dollar too. It was time to do some good. I wanted to be prepared.

I left for school as usual. But I didn't walk in that direction. Instead, I walked to the rec center. I crossed the soccer fields. I walked up the path toward the duplex.

The same window was still up around back. I looked around. Then pulled myself up. I dropped into a bedroom. Started for the door.

I had forgotten a major rule. About checking for dogs.

Big mistake!

CHAPTER 12

TELL THE TRUTH

A huge dog charged me. Looked like it wanted to eat me for breakfast. The dog snarled. Showed its teeth. Took a step closer.

I felt the wall behind me. I was trapped.

The dog kept its eyes on me. After a while, it sat. I tried to slide across the wall toward the window. It stood up again. Growled. I stopped moving.

Options? Yelling wouldn't do me any good. There weren't any neighbors to hear me. On one

side was a vacant house. On the other were playing fields.

I doubted anyone would even walk by. It was
Monday morning. Most kids were in school. Sure
wished I had gone too.

I slid down the wall to sit on the floor. The
dog's muscles tensed, but it didn't move.

Would this dog let me use the bathroom? As
soon as I thought of it, I needed to go. I looked at
the bedroom door. The dog growled.

"Nice doggy," I said. "Nice, nice doggy."

The dog wasn't fooled. It just kept staring at
me.

I looked away. Didn't feel like having a staring contest with a dog. I checked out the bedroom.
It was a wreck. There was a big hole in the wall. It
looked like someone had punched it.

There was a dresser and a bed. That was all.
One leg of the dresser was missing. Someone had
propped it up with a block. It was lower than the
other three legs. It tilted at a funny angle.

The mirror above the dresser was cracked.

The bed didn't have any sheets on it. It was just a bare mattress. A blanket was bunched up at the foot of the bed. The pillow was stained. There was no pillowcase.

Out of the corner of my eye, I saw something move. The biggest roach I'd ever seen crossed the floor. Even the dog noticed. We both watched it for a while. Then the dog went back to watching me.

What had I been thinking? I didn't know why I had broken in. Even from the outside the place was a dump. I really wished I had kept my vow to quit.

Being here was torture. The place was disgusting. My apartment was way nicer than this. I didn't want to trade lives with this person. Whoever lived here should trade lives with me!

After what seemed like forever, I heard the front door open. Loud voices were arguing. A man and a woman.

"But I never—" the man said.

"I'm tired of your lies!" the woman shouted. "You let me in this instant! I'm looking around. I know you're not alone in here."

Well, this was going to be interesting. I stood up. Didn't want to have to explain why I was there.

The dog ran out of the room. Its tail was wagging.

As soon as it was gone, I ran to the window. Swung one leg over the sill. Caught my jeans on a nail. Wiggled myself free. I shifted my weight to swing my other leg over.

All of a sudden, the woman burst through the bedroom door. She stopped short when she saw me. It was Bernice!

I could see her try to work out who I was.

The guy behind her couldn't stop in time. He bumped into her. I don't think she even noticed.

This dude was Michael. Had to be. Same guy who was in Bernice's apartment.

She had a really puzzled look on her face. "How do I know you?" she asked.

The man pushed her out of the way. He lunged for my arm. "You're not going anywhere," he said. He pulled hard.

I lost my balance. Tipped over into the room. Fell to the floor.

"It's him!" the man shouted. "The kid who cleaned the apartment!"

God, it was Michael. I was in so much trouble.

Bernice still looked confused. "Wait," she said, looking down at me. "Aren't you Monique Davis's son?"

I nodded miserably.

"What's he doing here?" she asked the man.

The guy was glaring at me. "You'll have to ask him," he said. "I don't know this kid. First time I saw him was in your apartment. Should've shot him, considering the mess he's made."

"Dwayne, right?" Bernice said.

I sat up. "Yeah," I answered.

"You'd better start at the beginning," Bernice said. She pulled the blanket up to cover the bare mattress. Then she sat down. "And you'd better tell the truth."

CHAPTER 13

I'M CALLING THE COPS

Are you Michael?" I asked the man.

He nodded.

"I didn't know this was your place," I said. "I didn't know the other place was yours either," I added.

"So why are you here?" Michael asked.

"I just—" What could I say? "I like being inside people's homes," I said. "Pretending their life is my life."

Bernice and Michael looked at me like I was crazy.

"Weren't you at the other place to meet your aunt?" Michael asked.

I shook my head. "I made that up to keep you from shooting me."

"But you cleaned the place," he said. "What was up with that?"

"I wanted to hang out there," I said. "But it was a mess. So I cleaned it up first. But then you came home."

"You just sit in people's homes?" Bernice asked. "You break in just to be there? I don't understand."

"I don't either. Not really," I said. "I like pretending it's my place. Stupid, I know."

"Dangerous is more like it," Michael said. "Did you take her ring?"

I nodded. "I wanted a souvenir," I said. "Something to remind myself of the day. I didn't think you'd miss it."

"That was my mother's wedding ring," Bernice said. "Where is it now?"

I put my hand in my pocket. Michael tensed up. The dog growled.

"Easy," I said to everyone. I pulled out the ring. "Here." I handed it to Bernice. "I'm really, really sorry."

"Wait a minute," Michael said. "How'd you end up in this place? You following me?"

"Dumb luck. I didn't know it was yours," I said, shaking my head. "I knew you lived over here somewhere. You mentioned that at dinner, remember?" I said to Bernice.

She nodded.

"I wanted to find you to give you back the ring," I said to Michael. "I looked for you on Saturday. Then I saw the open window here."

"So you hit me twice?" Michael asked.

I nodded. Shrugged. It was nuts.

"Why did you pick my apartment the last time?" Bernice asked.

"There was a ladder against the building," I explained. "Can't seem to resist things like that."

Michael reached for his pocket. I tensed. Wondered if he was going to pull out his gun. Instead, he pulled out a phone.

"I'm calling the cops," Michael said. "I want this little thief gone."

"No!" I pleaded. "Please! I'll do anything. Just …" I stopped.

"What?" Bernice asked.

"Don't call the cops. And don't tell my mother," I begged.

Bernice looked at Michael. He shook his head.

"No," he said. "I'm not doing you any favors. You messed up my life. My girl thought I was lying. Thought I was cheating on her. I lost my girl and my home."

Bernice moved a little closer to Michael. She laced her fingers through his.

"And for what? To borrow somebody else's life?" Michael said. "Why would you want anybody else's life? Why would you want to trade your life for this?" He made a sweeping motion with his hand.

I shrugged. Couldn't explain it. What was wrong with my life?

"There is something," Bernice said slowly. "I might be inclined to keep this from your mom. But in exchange—"

"Anything," I said quickly. "It would kill her to know."

"This place could stand to be cleaned," she said. "Top to bottom. Ceiling to floor. Cleaned till it shines."

"Wait a minute," Michael said. "I don't want this kid here a minute longer!"

"This place needs a good cleaning," Bernice said to him. "So your landlord can rent it to someone else. You don't need to live here anymore." She kissed him on the cheek.

"Really?" he said, grinning.

I was glad Bernice forgave him. "Okay, that's

great," I said. I stood up. "How about eleven on Saturday?" I didn't want Bernice to change her mind.

"Not so fast," she said, turning back to me. "We need to get something straight about your mom. I'm not going to tell her. Yet. But know this. You do one thing wrong and I tell." She leaned forward. "Are you hearing me? Stay out of trouble. Go to school. Do your homework."

I nodded.

"Your mom talks about you a lot," Bernice continued. "Brags about you. She ever tells me you did something wrong? I tell her about this. This will hang over you till the day you die. Got it?"

"Got it," I said. A life sentence of being good. But better than the alternatives. Michael calling the cops. Bernice telling my mom. I wasn't sure which was worse.

I stood up. Turned to Michael. "I'm really, really sorry." I stuck my hand out. "I'm Dwayne, by the way. Dwayne Davis."

"Michael Stevens," he said, shaking my hand. "Don't expect me to forgive you right away. It's going to take a while."

"I know," I said. "But thanks anyway."

I headed for the window.

"How about you use the door? This way," Michael said. He led me through the living room. I looked around.

He had a really nice couch. A good TV.

Maybe when I was done cleaning, I could sit a little while.

CHAPTER 14

THE WATCH

My list of good things that happened today.

1. I was still alive
2. Michael didn't shoot me
3. Bernice got her ring back
4. Michael and Bernice got back together
5. I still felt the rush of breaking and entering
6. Oh yeah, the dog didn't bite me

My hobby was beyond risky. It was wrong. I could die. But it was becoming a habit. I needed to become legit. Get a job that gets me into people's homes. Legally.

My list of possible jobs.

Locksmith

Cable TV installer

Painter

Plumber

I walked home and pulled out my phone. Called the number from the sign. On the light pole. A man answered.

"I think I have something of yours," I said.

"Yeah? Describe it," he said.

"Gold rim. Scratched glass. Black leather band," I said.

"Sounds like it," the man said. "Want to tell me where you got it?"

Tell him the truth? Heck no. I couldn't do it. "Not really," I said. "I just want to give it back."

"I suppose you're looking for the reward," he said.

For a moment I hesitated. Might be nice. But that would be mean. Steal the watch and get a reward for returning it? That was pretty low.

"Nah," I said. "I'll just give it to you. Where can we meet?"

The guy was quiet for a moment. "Where are you now?" he asked.

I looked around. "On Spruce Street. Near where you posted that sign." *Near your apartment*, I thought.

I couldn't tell him I knew where he lived. He probably assumed I stole the watch. I didn't want to admit to it.

"There's a 7-Eleven where Spruce meets Bigelow Boulevard," he said. "I can be there in about thirty minutes."

"I know that 7-Eleven," I said. "I'll wait for you there. How will I know you?"

"I'll have on a red shirt," he said. "How about you?"

I looked down. I was wearing a black T-shirt. "I have on a green plaid shirt," I lied.

"See you soon," he said. "And, son?"

I waited.

"Thank you," he said. "That watch means everything to me."

I hung up. Walked toward the store. Walked inside. I poured myself a Slurpee. I put my hand in my pocket. Felt the watch and the coin.

I was about to give back the watch. That only left the coin. Somehow I would have to give that back too.

I got in line at the cash register. Handed over my money. Went outside. Then I heard sirens. Didn't think too much about them. There always seem to be sirens in the city.

It was hot. But the Slurpee cooled me down. Yum! Oh man! I realized why. He'd called the cops.

I dropped the drink in a trash can on the street. Forced myself not to run. Walked down Bigelow. All cool and calm.

At the next corner I looked back. Three cop cars had pulled into the parking lot. They'd be looking for someone in a green plaid shirt. I was so glad I'd lied.

But I was mad. No questions asked? That was bull. He almost got me arrested. And the cops would have asked lots of questions.

I walked back toward his apartment. There was the darn sign. It was attached with some heavy tape. I pulled the tape up. Took out the watch. Stuck it under the tape. Pulled out my phone.

He answered on the first ring.

"I should just keep this watch," I said. " 'No questions asked.' And then you call the cops. You don't deserve to get this back."

"Son, you broke into my apartment. I hardly think you should lecture me," the man said.

"You want this watch? Look under your sign. The one by your apartment," I said. "I'm done with it."

CHAPTER 15

THE OLD LADY

I still had the silver dollar. The last thing to return. I headed toward the old lady's apartment.

I thought back to the morning I broke in. I remembered seeing a young couple leave. They looked like they were going to the office.

Now it was afternoon. I hoped they were still working. I was done explaining myself.

There was another problem. My cell phone. Had to get rid of it. Because of the watch guy. I'd called him twice. He had my number. I could be traced.

He had already called the cops once. Nothing to stop him from calling them again. They could trace my cell. They could find me easily.

Ditching my phone sucked. But I had no choice.

Put it on a mailbox. Someone would pick it up. Probably within the hour.

I'd tell my mother I'd lost it. Same thing to the cops if they came around. More lies.

No way would my mom buy me another phone. She'd make me work for it. I didn't mind. Much better than going to juvie.

Now for the old lady. I walked right up to the building's front door. Pulled it open. Whoever had used the door last hadn't latched it. Lame. Pushed it shut behind me.

Click.

Now that was how it was supposed to be closed. People can be so careless.

I found the old lady's apartment. Knocked. Didn't hear anything. Then *thump*. Followed by a shuffle. *Thump*. And shuffle. It was her. Using her walker.

I waited outside the door. I knew she was looking through the peephole. I held up the coin. "This is yours," I said. "I want to return it."

She didn't say anything.

"Ma'am? I know you're there. And I know you can hear me," I said. "I'm really, really sorry. I shouldn't have taken this. It's the only thing I took. I swear it."

I bent down. Put the coin on her doormat. Stood back up.

"I left it on the mat," I said. "I'm leaving now. After I'm gone you can get it. Goodbye."

I gave the peephole a little wave. I turned and walked out of the building.

What a wild ride. Now everything was right again.

I returned everything I had stolen. Nobody

ended up being hurt by what I'd done. Not even Michael.

Not even me.

I walked down the street toward my apartment. I needed to cross the street before my block. I looked to my right. I could see the back of a building.

The light changed. I started to go across. Then I hesitated. Looked again.

A window at the back of the building was open. It was up a couple of inches.

I gave myself a shake. I was done breaking and entering. There was no way I was going to go in.

I crossed the street. Then I turned at the corner. Headed toward the rec center. Maybe Q, Alex, and Jordan were playing ball.

It wouldn't hurt to check it out. Play a pickup game.

WANT TO KEEP READING?

9781680211047

Turn the page for a sneak
peek at another book in the
White Lightning series:

SCRATCH N' SNITCH

CHAPTER 1

ME, ME, AND ME

Mia Gonzalez walked over to the "cool" bench. You had to be cool to hang there. She saw Cassidy and Nicole. They were her besties at Marina Middle School. The cool bench was in the center of campus. The girls stood there so everybody could see them. They were picture-perfect. Always.

The three girls were the coolest eighth graders at school. Mia was a goddess, with her long brown hair and tanned skin. Cassidy and Nicole made her shine. Both had blonde hair and fair skin. Mia "popped" in between.

The three girls got straight As. They didn't have to study hard. Or work much.

Mia was the most popular. Kids envied Cassidy and Nicole. But Mia had a way about her that went beyond them.

Mia knew she was cool. And that wasn't a good thing.

She was spoiled.

She was self-centered.

She was selfish.

She was just about every bad "self" word you could be.

She had been popular since first grade. Nobody challenged her. Everybody accepted how she was.

Mia got within a few feet of the cool bench. Deemed cool by her, naturally. She saw something that made her jaw drop. Two boys were standing next to it. Her bench! They were too close for comfort.

"What's up with the losers?" she asked Cassidy and Nicole.

As usual, the girls had their phones. They were always holding them. Always taking selfies. And posting. They *were* their phones.

"We thought we'd let you handle it." Cassidy grinned. Then she checked her phone.

"Yeah, you're better at dealing with losers than we are," Nicole said.

"I know." Mia smiled smugly.

She walked over to the two boys. They wore hoodies. Skinny jeans. Vans. They had long hair. And they held skateboards.

All Mia saw were two kids who were less than she was.

Less good-looking. Less popular. Less smart. Why? Because she thought they were.

"Gross," Mia said when she got closer. "Why don't you two take your discussion somewhere else." It wasn't a question.

They both stared at her.

"You're too close to the cool bench." She pointed to it. Rolled her eyes. Cassidy and Nicole giggled.

"We're not even near—" one boy started to say.

"Listen," Mia snapped. "I'm person. You're a person. But I'm a *better* person. Everybody knows this bench is ours. So, why don't you two go somewhere else? Sit at the lunch tables with the other skaters."

The boys had no reply. They stared at Mia. Then they walked away.

Mia sniffed. Mission accomplished. She noticed some posters for the Zombie Dance that Friday. The school hosted the dance the week before Halloween every year. Mia and her boyfriend, Neil, hadn't talked about going. They didn't have to. She knew he would take her.

Neil went to Ocean High School. He was one of the few sophomores on the varsity football team. He was tall. And he looked like a surfer, with a muscular build and wavy blond hair.

Mia turned to Cassidy and Nicole. She was grinning as her phone buzzed with an incoming text. She knew it was Neil. He always texted her first thing in the morning.

NEIL: (Hang out later?)
MIA: (Maybe.)

She figured they would hang out. She wanted to. But she didn't want to seem too eager. Mia knew guys liked girls more when they had to work for it. Chase them.

"Who was that?" Cassidy asked.

"Neil." Mia shrugged. She liked not caring. Or at least looking like she didn't care.

The bell rang.

"Time to be bored." Mia rolled her eyes.

The girls followed her. They had classes in

the opposite direction. But they always walked Mia to her first class.

As they went, it seemed like all eyes were on them. Students moved out of their way. The girls liked parading around the campus.

They did get smiles from Rand, Donovan, and Jeff as they passed. They were eighth graders too. They liked to dress preppy—1980s all the way. They wore topsiders. Polo shirts. Dress pants. They even combed their hair like guys did in the '80s. They were as popular as Mia, Cassidy, and Nicole.

Then the Scabs walked by.